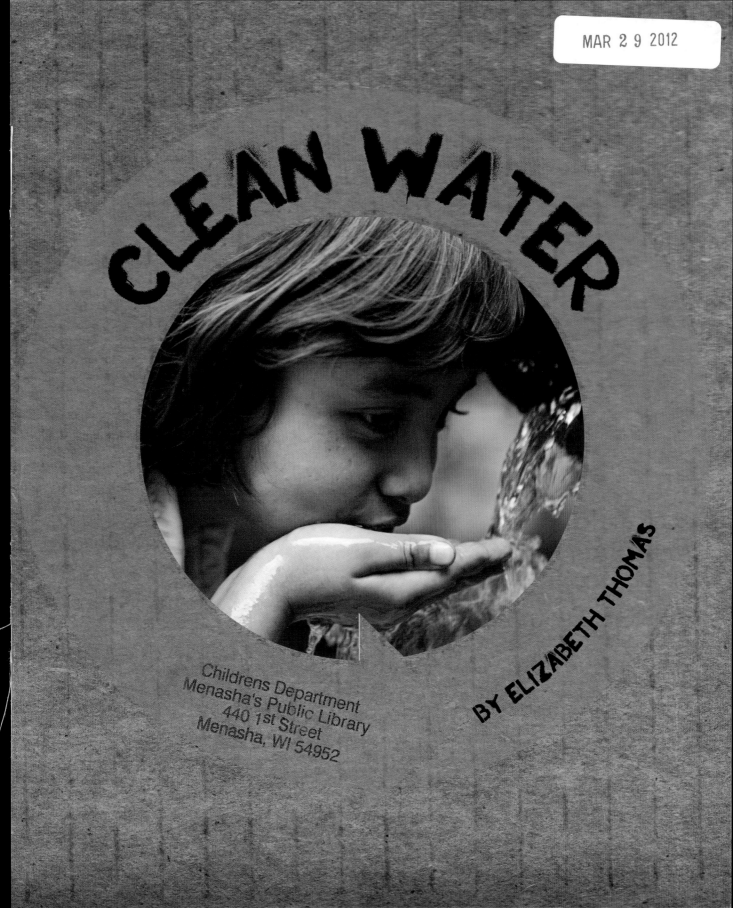

CLEAN WATER

BY ELIZABETH THOMAS

Published by The Child's World®
1980 Lookout Drive • Mankato, MN 56003-1705
800-599-READ • www.childsworld.com

PHOTO CREDITS
Bartosz Hadyniak/iStockphoto, cover, 1; S. Greg Panosian/iStockphoto, 5;
Shutterstock Images, 7, 25, 29; Fernando Carniel Machado/iStockphoto, 9;
Geoffrey Kuchera/Shutterstock Images, 11; Eleonora Kolomiyets/Shutterstock
Images, 13; Joe Gough/Shutterstock Images, 15; Alexander Raths/
iStockphoto, 17; iStockphoto, 19, 27; Olga Anourina/iStockphoto, 21;
Chanyut Sribua-rawd/iStockphoto, 23

CONTENT CONSULTANT
Jacques Finlay, Associate Professor, Department of Ecology,
Evolution and Behavior, University of Minnesota

ACKNOWLEDGMENTS
The Child's World®: Mary Berendes, Publishing Director
The Design Lab: Design
Red Line Editorial: Editorial direction

ISBN: 978-1-60973-171-7
LCCN: 2011927670

Printed in the United States of America in Mankato, MN
July, 2011
PA02090

TABLE OF CONTENTS

WHY CARE ABOUT CLEAN WATER?

Most of Earth is covered with water. But only 1 percent of the planet's water is freshwater we can drink. We also use this water for bathing, cooking, and many more activities.

This water can get polluted in many ways. Sometimes factories dump waste into streams. Chemical **fertilizers** wash into our water supplies. When forests are cut down carelessly, the roots that once held soil in place are gone. The soil washes away and ends up clogging our streams and lakes.

By keeping these harmful substances out of water, our water will stay clean. Another way to keep our water clean is to make sure we are not wasting it. Saving water helps save energy because it takes energy to keep water fresh and clean. Every time you keep water from running down the drain, you are helping save the planet's clean water supply!

Almost everyone can do something to help keep our water clean. It's easy and fun!

BE CAREFUL HOW YOU WATER

It's okay to water your lawn to make it nice and green. Just make sure you do it in a smart way. Make sure the sprinkler is placed on a dry part of the lawn. That way you will be watering only the parts of the lawn that need it. Also, check that the sprinkler is watering the lawn only. The street, sidewalk, and house do not need to be watered.

WHY?

Watering only the lawn will make sure water isn't wasted on streets and sidewalks that don't need to be watered. The extra water that goes into the lawn will go back into the **groundwater**, too.

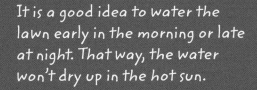

It is a good idea to water the lawn early in the morning or late at night. That way, the water won't dry up in the hot sun.

RYAN'S WELL

When Ryan Hreljiac was six years old, his teacher told the class about children in Uganda who did not have clean water to drink. Ryan wanted to help. He raised $2,000 to build a well that would give the children clean drinking water. Now that he is older, he has started Ryan's Well Foundation. It is committed to delivering freshwater to people all over the world.

FAUCET OFF WHILE BRUSHING

Save water twice a day with just a flick of your wrist. Turn the water off when you're brushing your teeth. Turn the water on only to rinse your toothbrush, your mouth, and the sink. When you brush this way, you **conserve** some of the planet's freshwater!

WHY?

You can save as much as 8 gallons (30 L) of water a day. Think of that as eight big jugs of milk. Even small drops leaking from a faucet can add up. This can waste from 9 to 20 gallons (34–76 L) a month! Turn off the water faucet tightly after each use.

Small changes to everyday things like brushing your teeth can add up to make a big difference!

TIP #3

GO FOR A WALK

On a nice weekend afternoon, ask your family to go for a walk along a riverbank or a beach. Pick up the litter as you go. Bring a couple bags for trash and a couple for recycling. Remember to wear gloves, too.

WHY?

Keeping beaches and riverbanks clean prevents trash and other materials from getting into water. Then they have less chance of harming the fish or other creatures that live in the water.

Keeping rivers, lakes, and streams clean helps humans and wildlife.

TIP #4

USE LESS TOILET WATER

Find two 16-ounce (448 mL) plastic bottles with screw-on caps. Pour an inch or two (2.5–5 cm) of sand or gravel into the bottles. Fill them up the rest of the way with water. Have a grown-up help you take the top off the toilet tank. Place the bottles inside the tank, away from the flushing parts. Put the lid back on the tank.

WHY?

The toilet is what uses the most water in each home. By making the toilet tank need less water to fill up, your family could save thousands of gallons of water every year.

Some older toilets can use as much as 7 gallons (26 L) of water per flush.

SHORT SHOWER

If you shorten your shower by just a minute or two, you could save up to 150 gallons (568 L) of water each month! Here's how to take a shorter shower:

1. Turn on the water and get wet.
2. Turn off the water. Soap your body and shampoo your hair.
3. Turn on the water and rinse off.

WHY?

If every single person in the United States took a shorter shower and saved just 1 gallon (3.8 L) of water a year, a lot of water would be saved. It would be twice the amount of freshwater pumped out of the Great Lakes for human use every day!

A long, hot shower uses a lot of water and energy.

WASHING DISHES

Don't keep the water on while you are washing dishes. Instead of letting the water run while you scrub the pots and pans, let them soak for a while. This will make cleaning them easier, too!

If you have a dishwasher, only run it when there is a full load of dirty dishes. Running the dishwasher with only a few dishes inside wastes water and energy. It also adds more soap into the water supply.

WHY?

By running water while doing dishes by hand, you may use more than 40 gallons (151 L) of clean water at a time. Modern dishwashers need less than 10 gallons (38 L) per load.

Load up the dishwasher! Only running it when it is full is one easy way to be smart about using water.

TIP #7

COLD WATER PITCHER

Cold water on a hot day is so great! Here's an idea: always keep a pitcher of water in the refrigerator. That way, you won't have to run the tap a few seconds until the water gets cold. Refill a few water bottles and keep them in the refrigerator. They'll be nice and cold, and you can take them with you.

WHY?

People use freshwater faster than it can be replaced naturally. Every drop of water we conserve means our rivers, lakes, and **reservoirs** will stay full of fresh, clean water longer. Then we won't run out.

Keeping cold water on hand helps prevent wasting water at the sink.

USE YOUR PET'S OLD WATER

There are a number of ways you can help save water when you take care of your pets. When you clean out the fish tank, don't throw the old water away! The water is full of nutrients. Use it to give a drink to your houseplants. When you give your pet freshwater in its bowl, don't throw the old water down the drain. Use it to water your garden and trees.

WHY?

Giving plants and trees the water that is naturally filled with nutrients means that they won't need as much fertilizer to help them grow. Some fertilizers get washed into rivers and streams and become **pollutants**.

If you don't finish drinking a glass of water, don't pour it down the sink. Use it to water a plant instead!

PLANT A TREE

Plant a tree! Trees are a beautiful way to help keep our water clean. The roots keep dirt from washing away. The bigger the tree grows, the deeper the roots are.

WHY?

Dirt that is not held in place can get washed into our storm sewers, which affects our water quality. By planting a tree, you are helping to keep the dirt in the ground where it belongs!

A tree's roots provide the tree with water and nutrients from the soil. They also help hold the soil in place.

JOIN A CLEAN TEAM

A watershed is an area of land that catches rain or snow and lets it seep into lakes, rivers, wells, marshes, or groundwater. Watersheds can be very large or just a few football fields in size. It's important to keep these watersheds as clean as we can. The Tennessee Water Authority has created teams of kids to help keep them clean. One team helped stop erosion on about 3,630 feet (1,106 m) of shoreline at local parks. They helped save land, water, and fish!

TIP #10

USE NATURAL FERTILIZER

Growing your own vegetables is a great way to go green. It lets you eat locally grown food instead of eating foods shipped from across the country to your grocery store. Just make sure you tend your garden in a way that keeps water clean. Use natural fertilizer! This can be manure or your family's own **compost**.

WHY?

Chemical fertilizers may seep into groundwater and then into a community's freshwater supply. Natural fertilizer is better for your plants and less likely to affect groundwater.

You can make your
own compost bin!
Ask an adult to help
you get started.

COMPOSTING

TIP #11

DO YOUR DUTY

Ask your teacher to help your class contact your public officials. Write letters encouraging them to support laws and programs to protect the water where you live. Suggest they look for ways to control pollution. Or, have everyone think of an idea to suggest to your lawmakers to help keep freshwater clean.

WHY?

A public official's job is to act on behalf of you and all the people in your community. They especially listen when they hear a lot of the same requests. The more letters your class sends, the more likely an official will make a change.

Write a letter to let your public officials know what issues are important to you.

USE A RAIN BARREL

Catch rainwater in a rain barrel. Ask a grown-up to help you with these steps:

1. Use a plastic garbage can or any other large barrel with a lid.
2. Put a spigot toward the bottom so you can get the water out.
3. Cut a hole in the top of the lid.
4. Position your rain barrel so that the hole in the lid is under the roof's downspout.

WHY?

A quarter-inch (.64 cm) of rain falling from the roof of a home is about 200 gallons (757 L) of water. In a downpour, your rain barrel could be filled in a few minutes! Use the water that collects to water your garden or plants on a sunny day. That way, you'll need less water from your community's water supply.

A rain barrel is a clever way to reuse water that falls on the roof.

MORE WAYS TO GO GREEN

1. **Have** your parents wash the car at a car wash that uses recycled water.

2. **Start** an environmental club at your school.

3. **Pick** up after your dog. This will prevent bacteria from making people, pets, or other animals sick.

4. **When** you are washing your hands, turn off the faucet while you are lathering.

5. **Wash** your fruits and vegetables in a pan of water instead of under running water from the tap.

6. **Collect** the water you used from rinsing fruit and vegetables and use it to water houseplants.

7. **Keep** one glass for your drinking water or refill a water bottle. This means fewer glasses to wash.

8. **While** the water is heating up for your shower, catch it in a bucket in the shower. You can use this water to water the garden.

9. **Whenever** you have leftover ice in your cup from a take-out restaurant, use it to give plants a cool drink. Hanging baskets outside would enjoy an icy drink as well!

10. **Never** pour chemicals down the sink or toilet. Chemicals we use every day—such as cleaning sprays, bug killers, or paints—need to be disposed of in special ways.

11. **When** you wash your bike, fill up a bucket with water. It will use much less water than running the hose!

12. **Share** these tips with your friends and classmates!

compost (KOM-pohst): Compost is a mixture of leaves, old food scraps, and soil that is used to fertilize plants and land. Compost is better for Earth than chemical fertilizer.

conserve (kun-SURV): To conserve means to save something from loss or waste. You can do your part to conserve water while you brush your teeth by turning off the faucet.

erosion (ih-ROH-zhun): Erosion is the gradual wearing away of soil by wind or water. Tree roots help stop erosion.

fertilizers (FUR-tuh-lyz-urs): Fertilizers are substances put on land to make it richer and to help plants or crops grow better. Fertilizers may or may not have chemicals.

groundwater (GROUND-wah-tur): Groundwater is water that is underground in soil or in crevices in rocks. Chemical fertilizers can seep into groundwater.

pollutants (puh-LOOT-unts): Pollutants are things that pollute. Chemical fertilizers can be pollutants.

reservoirs (REZ-ur-vwars): Reservoirs are natural or human-made areas that store large amounts of water. Conserving water keeps reservoirs fuller for longer periods of time.

watershed (WAH-tur-shed): A watershed is an area of land that separates waters flowing to different rivers or oceans. A watershed may collect rain or snow and let it seep into a variety of water storage places.

FURTHER READING

BOOKS

Donald, Rhonda Lucas. *Water Pollution*. New York:
Children's Press, 2001.

Geiger, Beth. *Sally Ride Science: Clean Water*. New York:
Roaring Brook Press, 2008.

Kelsey, Elin. *Not Your Typical Book About the Environment*.
Toronto: Owlkids Books, 2010.

WEB SITES

Visit our Web site for links about clean water:
http://www.childsworld.com/links

Note to Parents, Teachers, and Librarians: We routinely verify our Web links to make
sure they are safe and active sites. So encourage your readers to check them out!